MY BUSY BEING BELLA DAY

For Susanna and my mother

MY BUSY BEING BELLA DAY
A JONATHAN CAPE BOOK 978 1 780 08007 9

Published in Great Britain by Jonathan Cape, an imprint of Random House Children's Publishers UK
A Random House Group Company

This edition published 2013

1 3 5 7 9 10 8 6 4 2

Copyright © Rebecca Patterson, 2013

The right of Rebecca Patterson to be identified as the author of this work has been
asserted in accordance with the Copyright, Designs and Patents Act 1988.

RANDOM HOUSE CHILDREN'S PUBLISHERS UK,
61–63 Uxbridge Road, London W5 5SA

www.**randomhousechildrens**.co.uk
www.**randomhouse**.co.uk

Addresses for companies within The Random House Group Limited can be found at:
www.randomhouse.co.uk/offices.htm

THE RANDOM HOUSE GROUP Limited Reg. No. 954009

A CIP catalogue record for this book is available from the British Library.

Printed in China

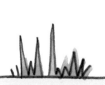

MIX
Paper from
responsible sources
FSC® C104723

The Random House Group Limited supports the Forest Stewardship Council®(FSC®),
the leading international forest certification organization. Our books carrying the FSC label are printed on
FSC®-certified paper. FSC is the only forest certification scheme endorsed by the leading environmental organizations,
including Greenpeace. Our paper procurement policy can be found at www.randomhouse.co.uk/environment.

MY BUSY BEING BELLA DAY

Rebecca Patterson

Jonathan Cape • London

Today I have to go to my nursery.
I will be **BUSY**. But what about **BOB**?

What will **HE**
do today?

After we have said,
"Good morning,
Mr Busy Bear!" we
have to colour in a 2 for
Margaret, working very hard
to do a really good job! But . . .

I DON'T THINK BOB'S WORKING TODAY!

At snack time,
I see Mummy has
given me a banana . . .

with **SPOTS!**
Sasha has kiwi slices in a special pot.
And Bob is probably . . .

in the café

LICKING FOAM.

At playtime, the house is full and Sasha is very, **VERY BUSY** playing jumping ponies with Sophie.

I bet Bob is at that place with the **CURLY SLIDE.**

After playtime, we make pictures. This pasta is

VERY HARD

to stick!

I WISH

I was at home with Bob!

Bob never has to stick

ANYTHING!

And Bob never has to sing
about **TEAPOTS** either.

Margaret says,
"Oh, well done, Bella.
I can hear every word!"

Margaret is right,

I AM THE
LOUDEST TEAPOT
HERE!

Later on at nursery, I get
a turn on the horses.

BOB WOULD NOT BE ALLOWED ON THIS!

He might wobble off!

At dressing-up time
I am a Fairy Queen Princess
and I need **A LOT**
of clothes.

Bob can't even put on a **SOCK!**

And then we shake those lentil shakers
we made last week.

SHAKE! SHAKE! SHAKE!

SHAKE! SHAKE!

Afterwards I tidy up
for Margaret, and I am

TOO BUSY

to think about Bob.

Then I am the

SPECIAL PERSON

who chooses the weather!

It is story time
and I am
tired.

What about **BOB?**

Is he having
a little nap
now?

At the end of nursery, I run out and shout:

HELLO!
HELLO BOB!
HELLO MUMMY!

I'VE BEEN SO BUSY!
BUT WHAT HAS BOB DONE TODAY?

Mummy says,
"We haven't done *anything* exciting.
Most of the time Bob was busy...

. . . missing you!"